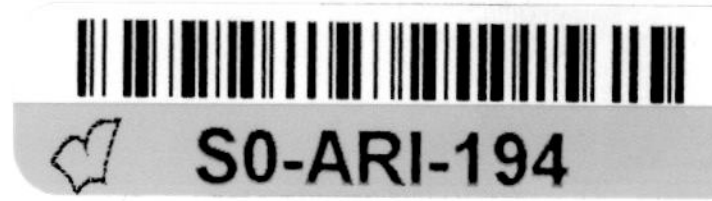

. . . for parents and teachers

Death, divorce, physical separation, and other forms of loss are all emotionally difficult experiences. They require all of our personal resources in working through our feelings.

For a young child, coping with the loss of a friend who is moving away can be just as difficult as coping with a more severe loss. It is crucial that children going through any such loss be able to express their attitudes and feelings.

My Best Friend Moved Away touches upon many of the emotions accompanying such an event. It provides an especially suitable background for the discussion of the feelings involved in any type of loss.

I encourage parents, teachers, and other professionals to facilitate the sharing of emotions through the sharing of this story.

MANUEL S. SILVERMAN, Ph.D.
ASSOCIATE PROFESSOR AND CHAIR
DEPARTMENT OF GUIDANCE
AND COUNSELING
LOYOLA UNIVERSITY OF CHICAGO

Trade Edition published 1992 © Steck-Vaughn Company

Library of Congress Number: 79-24111

11 12 13 95 94

Library of Congress Cataloging in Publication Data

Zelonky, Joy.
My best friend moved away.

SUMMARY: When his best friend moves away, Brian tries to cope with his feelings of loss and separation.
[1. Friendship — Fiction] 2. Moving, Household —Fiction] I. Adams, Angela. II. Title.
PZ7.Z398My [Fic] 79-24111
ISBN 0-8172-1353-8 hardcover library binding
ISBN 0-8114-7157-8 softcover binding

MY BEST FRIEND MOVED AWAY

by Joy Zelonky

illustrated by Angela Adams

introduction by Manuel S. Silverman, Ph.D.

Austin, Texas

I was starting to get worried about Nick. I waited and waited at the corner where we were supposed to meet, but there was no sign of him. If we were late again, I just knew Mrs. Hernandez was going to make us stay after school.

I especially didn't want Nick to be late for school. Some of the kids tease him about being slow because he has to wear a leg brace. I think Nick gets around better than just about anyone else I know.

Finally I saw him coming toward me. He looked ready to burst with excitement.

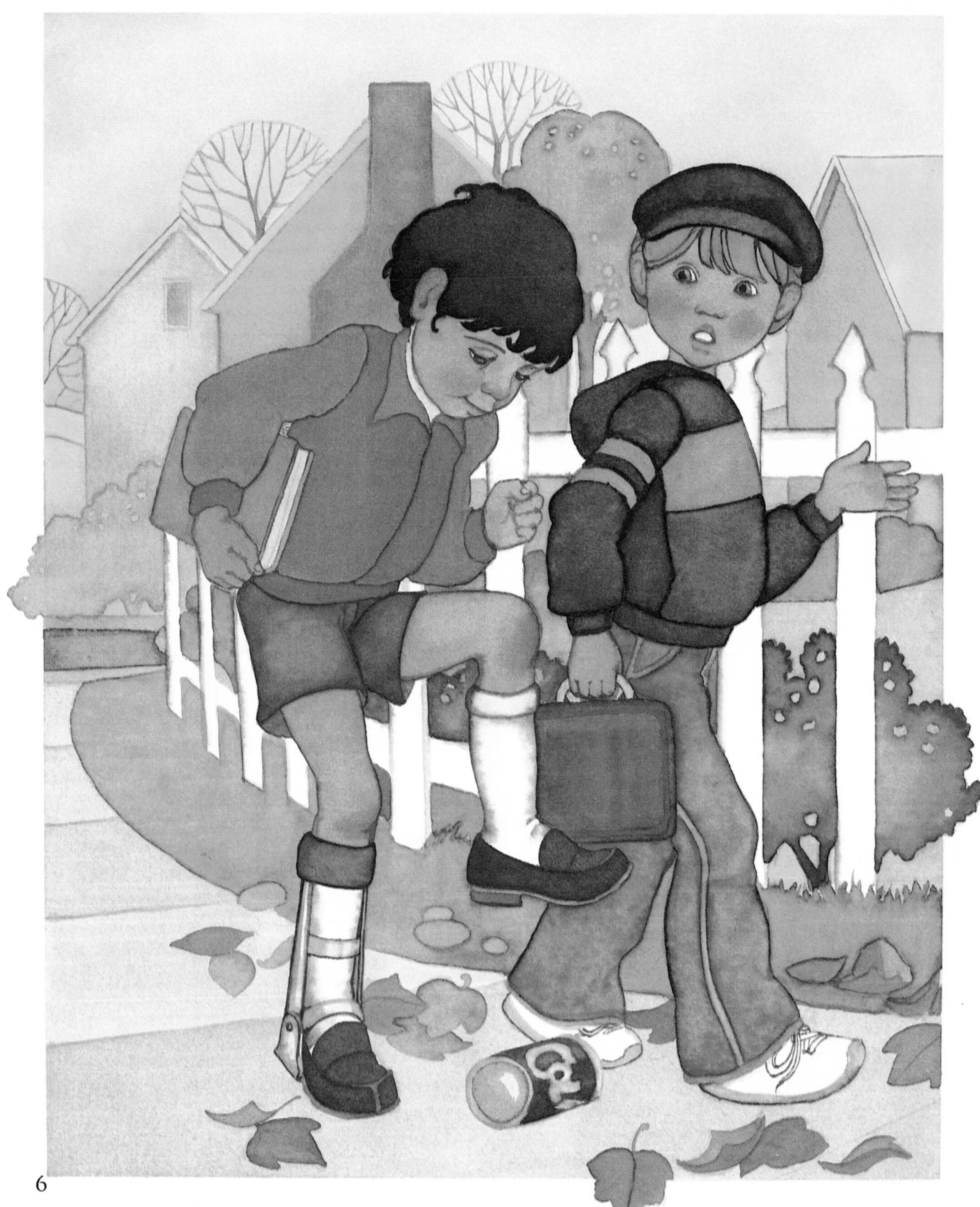

"Guess what!" Nick shouted. "My mom and dad bought a new house!"

I just stared at him for a minute. Then I asked, "Why did they do that?"

He came up to me, and we started walking toward school.

"Because our house isn't big enough," he said.

"I like your house. It looks a lot like ours."

"I like it too," Nick said. "It's just too small. My mom's having a baby soon. We need more room."

I wasn't sure I liked Nick's news, but I didn't want to tell him that. "Does that mean we can't walk to school together anymore?" I asked.

"Oh, I won't even be going to this school. Our new house is across town. I'm going to another school in a few weeks."

Now I was positive that I didn't like Nick's news. I couldn't stop thinking about it all day. Nick was my best friend. How could he move away? It didn't seem fair.

After school, Nick and I walked home together, as usual.

"Do you want to shoot some marbles?" I asked.

"I can't," he said. "Some people are coming over to look at our house tonight. I have to clean my room before they come."

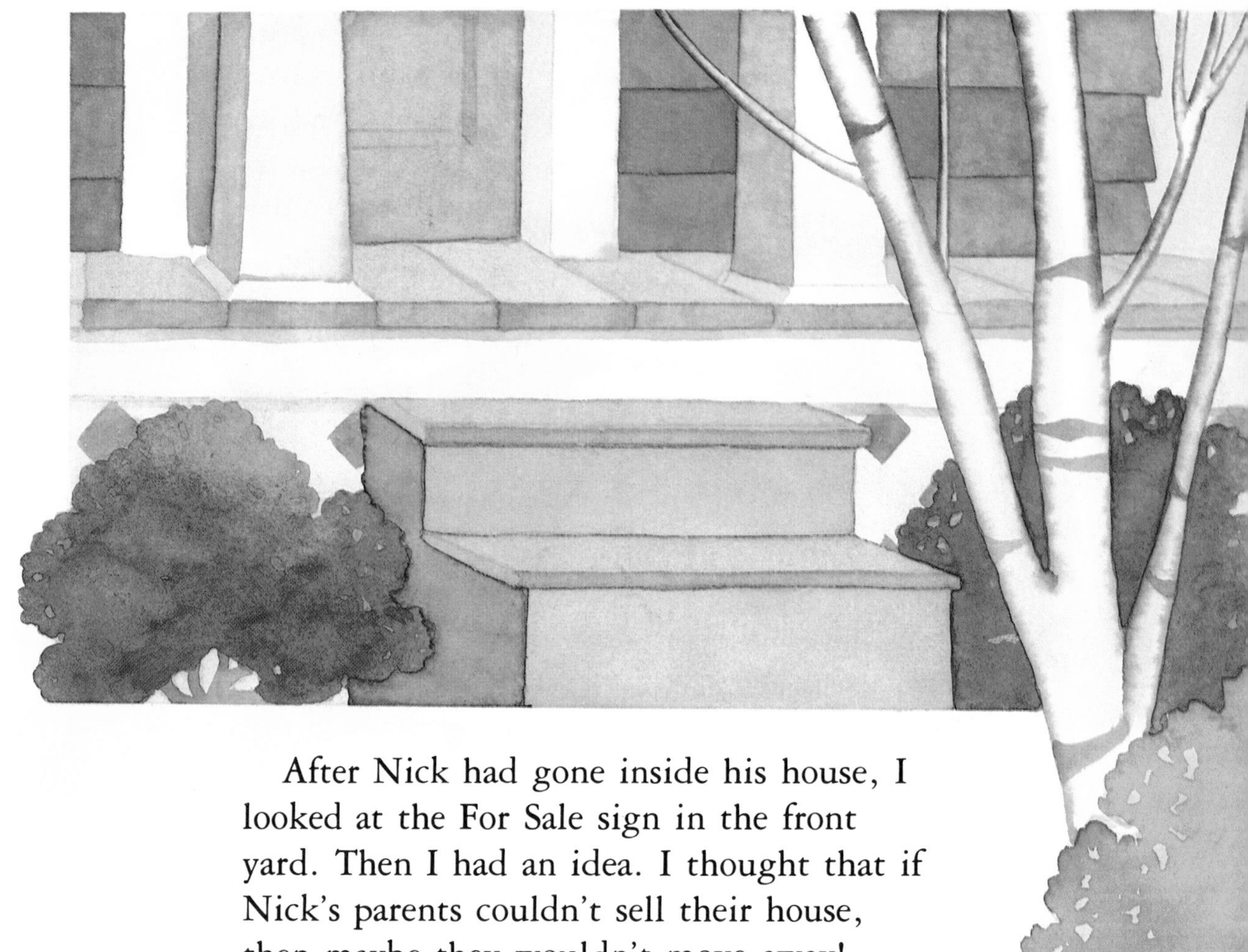

After Nick had gone inside his house, I looked at the For Sale sign in the front yard. Then I had an idea. I thought that if Nick's parents couldn't sell their house, then maybe they wouldn't move away!

Carefully I looked up and down the block. The only person on the whole street was the girl who delivers the papers.

After the girl had gone on to the next street, I crept over to the sign. I ripped the sign off its post and threw it as far as I could. Then I ran all the way home.

The next morning, Nick met me on the corner.

"Did you sell your house?" I asked, trying to act like I hoped the answer was yes.

"Maybe," Nick said. "The people liked it. But they almost didn't show up."

I felt my face turning red. "What do you mean?"

"Someone took our For Sale sign and threw it in the street. What a dirty trick! My dad finally found it and put it back up just in time."

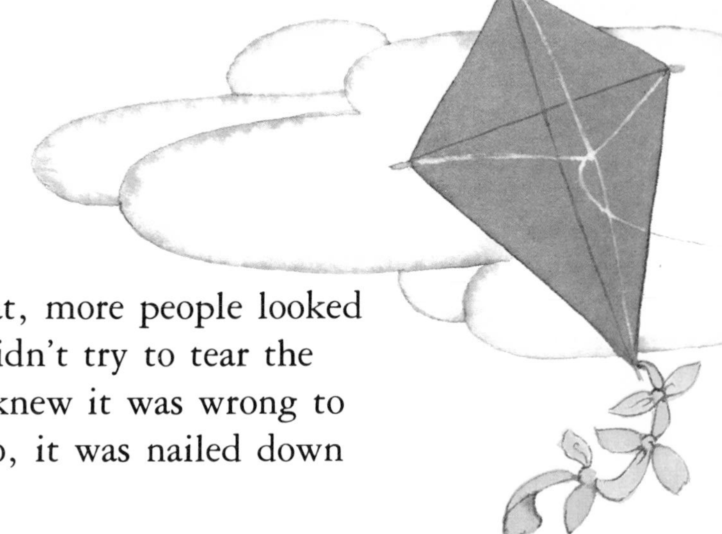

Each day after that, more people looked at Nick's house. I didn't try to tear the sign down again. I knew it was wrong to have done that. Also, it was nailed down too tightly.

One morning Nick was already at the corner when I got there.

"We sold our house!" he called.

"That's nice." Nick looked so happy that I just couldn't tell him how miserable I felt. "When are you moving?" I asked.

"Not for a month. That gives us plenty of time to play!"

After that, Nick and I did something together almost every day. Sometimes we played games with other kids, but usually it was just Nick and me.

We traded all of our comic books back and forth. We flew kites and sailed boats in the park. When it rained, we stayed inside and built forts out of blankets. We played a million games of marbles.

Then came moving day.

I went over to Nick's to say good-bye.

Nick waved from the car and said, "I wish you were moving too."

I took a small bag out of my pocket and handed it to him. "I . . . I want you to have these for a going-away present."

Nick's eyes grew wide. "Marbles," he whispered. "But these are your best ones."

"You're my best friend," I answered.

"Thanks, Brian. When you come over, you can use them, okay?"

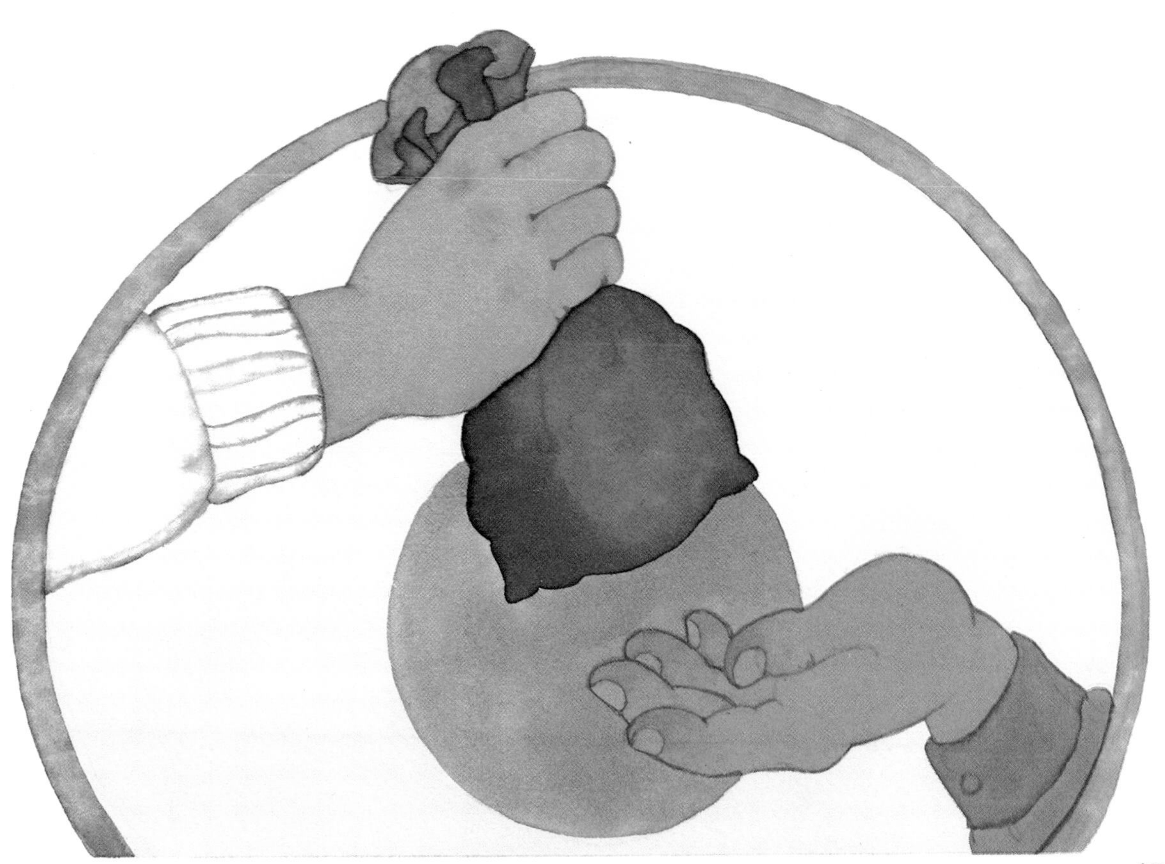

I nodded, waved good-bye, and went home. I sat on my bed and looked at the ceiling for a long time. I had never felt so bad. It was worse than the time my bicycle was stolen. At least that hadn't made me *lonely.*

Finally my dad came in and sat on the bed with me. "It's hard to be the one left behind, isn't it?" he said. "I'm sure you'll make new friends."

Dad didn't understand at all. "I'll never have a friend like Nick," I told him.

"You're right," he said. "No two people are alike. That's why each friend is special."

Dad was right about Nick being special. I just about died of loneliness during the next few weeks. Then Nick called me and invited me to his new house.

My dad and I took the subway across town. He went on to do some shopping while I visited Nick.

"Come on!" said Nick. "I want to show you my room."

Nick's room was large and very nice. I was a little jealous.

After showing me around, Nick asked, "What do you want to do now?"

"How about flying a kite?"

"That's for babies," said Nick. "None of the kids around here do that."

"Then let's shoot marbles."

Nick shook his head. "That's dumb too. I'll tell you what — if you promise to keep it a secret, I'll take you somewhere really great."

I said okay, and Nick led me outside. We walked around the corner to an area where a new house was being built.

I looked around. "This looks kind of dangerous," I said.

"You sound just like my mom," Nick scoffed. "All the kids come here. It's fun — watch!"

Nick walked all the way across a board that stretched over a big hole. "Follow the leader," he called back to me.

I looked down. Muddy water filled the bottom of the hole.

"Chicken!" yelled Nick.

I took a deep breath and started across. Every time I took a step, the board wiggled. I tried to keep my balance by leaning from side to side. I wondered how Nick could possibly have done this with his leg brace. He must have practiced a lot. . . .

Splash! Down I fell.

"Are you all right?" asked Nick.

"I think so," I said shakily. I was too scared and wet to say much else.

"We'd better go back," Nick said. "You're no good at this."

Nick's mother took one look at us and knew where we'd been. She helped me clean up.

"Nick, I warned you not to play there," she said. "Brian could have been hurt, and you too. Maybe you'll learn to listen to me if you stay home all day tomorrow."

"Oh, Mom," Nick said. Then he turned to me. "It's all your fault. Now I can't do things with my friends tomorrow!"

I stared at Nick for a minute. Then I ran outside and met my dad on the sidewalk.

"What happened?" he asked. "Did you and Nick have a fight?"

"No, but Nick is so different now. He's not like the old Nick at all." The rest of the way to the subway, I explained what had happened.

"I bet Nick's not as happy as you think he is," said my dad. "This must be a hard time for him too. He has to make friends in a strange place. He has to get used to a new school. Everything's changed for him. Nick's changed too."

AVENUE

I tried looking at things from Nick's point of view and had to admit my dad was right.

"But why did he have to change?" I asked. "I liked Nick the way he was."

"The people you know won't always stay the same," he answered. "Sometimes all you can do is remember the good times you've shared."

I looked at my reflection in the subway window. "Will I change too?"

"What do you think?"

"I guess I will. But if I'm careful, maybe the good things about me will get better."

Suddenly I stood up. "Hey, Dad, could we get off now?"

"But it's not our stop yet."

"I know," I said. "But there's a good store that has marbles right here. I promised some kids down the block that I'd play marbles, and I gave all of my good ones to Nick, and —"

"Let's go!" said my dad.

S0-ACR-574

Deena's Lucky Penny

by Barbara deRubertis
Illustrated by Joan Holub and Cynthia Fisher

The Kane Press
New York

Book Design/Art Direction: Roberta Pressel

Library of Congress Cataloging-in-Publication Data

DeRubertis, Barbara.
Deena's lucky penny/by Barbara deRubertis; illustrated by Joan Holub and Cynthia Fisher.
p. cm. — (Math matters.)
Summary: While pondering how to buy her mother a birthday present with no money, Deena finds a penny and follows a process of discovery about how pennies add up to nickels, which add up to dimes, all the way up to four quarters making a dollar.
ISBN 1-57565-091-6 (pbk. : alk. paper)
[1. Money—Fiction. 2. Birthdays—Fiction.] I. Holub, Joan, ill. II. Fisher, Cynthia ill. III. Title. IV. Series.
PZ7.D4475De 1999
[E]—dc21
98-51117
CIP
AC

10 9 8 7

First published in the United States of America in 1999 by The Kane Press.
Printed in Hong Kong.

MATH MATTERS is a registered trademark of The Kane Press

www.kanepress.com

Deena had a problem—a big problem. Her mom's birthday was coming. But Deena didn't have any money to buy a present.

Not one penny.

Just then Deena saw something shiny in the grass. A penny! She picked it up. The penny felt warm in her hand. "Wow!" she said.

"What's up, Deena?" called Mrs. Green from next door.

“Look what I found!” Deena said.

“Oh! A lucky penny!” said Mrs. Green. “Do you know this rhyme, Deena?”

Find a penny.
Pick it up.
All the day you’ll have good luck.

"How can a penny be lucky?" asked Deena.

"I'll show you," said Mrs. Green. She pulled a handful of coins out of her pocket. "I'll give you four more pennies to go with your penny. How much money do you have now?"

"1, 2, 3, 4, 5 cents," said Deena. "That's the same as a nickel. Thanks, Mrs. Green!"

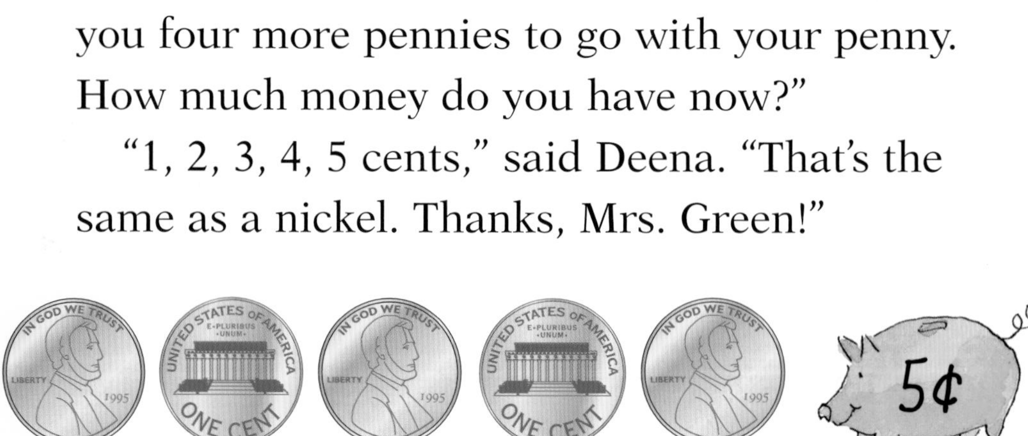

"Which would you rather have?" asked Mrs. Green. "Five pennies or a nickel?"

"A nickel, please!" said Deena. She traded Mrs. Green the five pennies for a nickel.

"Hey, Deena!" a voice called.

$1¢ + 1¢ + 1¢ + 1¢ + 1¢ = 5¢$

It was her brother, Sam, pedaling back from his paper route.

"Look, Sam! I found a lucky penny," Deena said. "Mrs. Green gave me four more pennies. Then she traded me a nickel for the pennies."

“That *was* a lucky penny!” Sam said. “What are you going to do with your five cents?”

“Save it,” Deena said. “Mom’s birthday is next week. I need money to buy a present.”

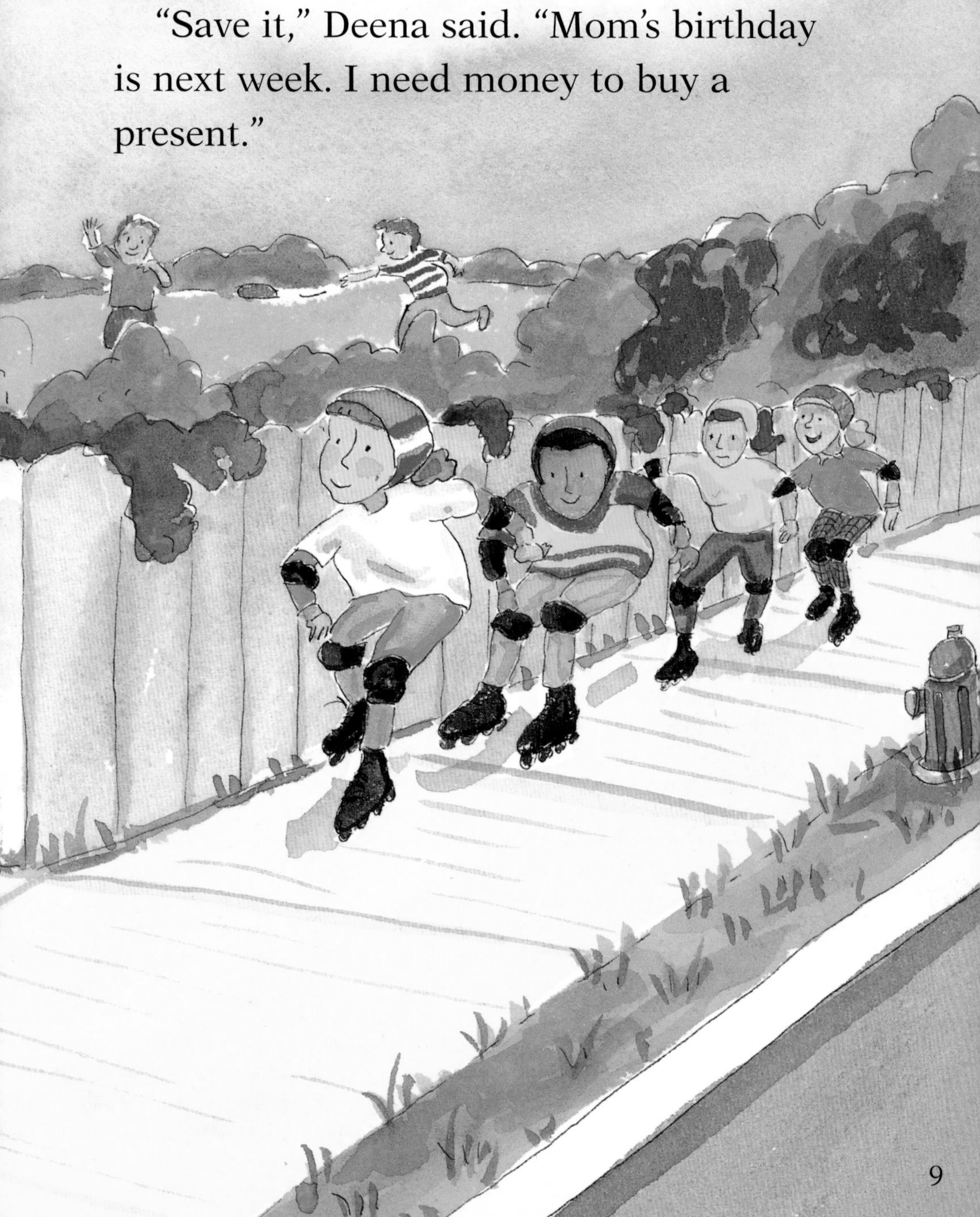

"I'll give you another nickel to go with that one." Sam pulled a nickel out of his pocket. "Now how much money do you have?"

"5 cents plus 5 cents equals 10 cents," said Deena. "That's the same as a dime! Thank you, Sam."

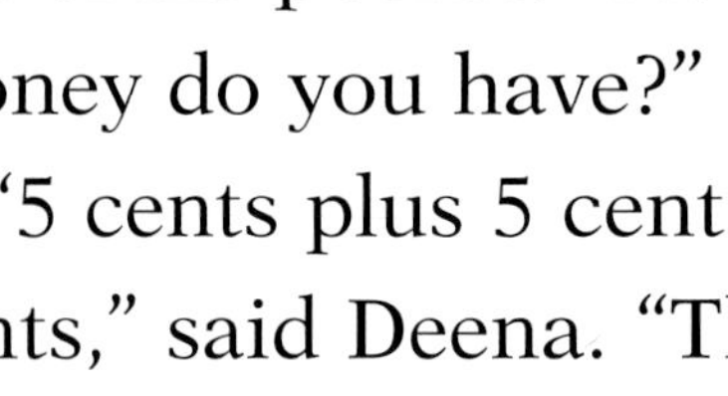

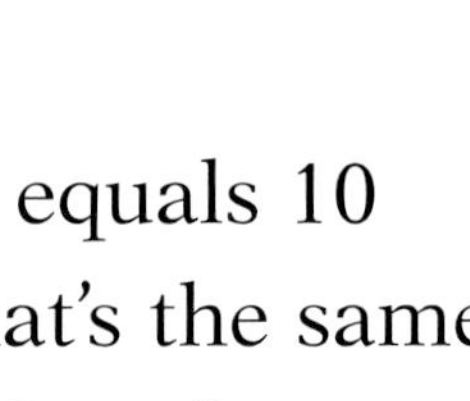

“Which would you rather have?” asked Sam. “Two nickels or one dime?”

“A dime,” said Deena.

They traded coins.

“It’s funny,” she said. “A dime is much smaller than a nickel, but it’s worth more!”

“Twice as much!” said Sam.

5¢ + 5¢ = 10¢

Deena's big sister Amy skated up to Deena.

"Listen, Amy," Deena said. "First I found a lucky penny. Then I got a nickel. And now I have a dime! I'm going to buy a present for Mom's birthday."

Amy smiled. "That dime looks lonely," she said. "I'd better give you another one."

"Thanks, Amy!" said Deena. "Now I have 10 cents plus 10 cents. That equals 20 cents. I'm going to show Dad!"

10¢ + 10¢ = 20¢

"Look, Dad! I found a lucky penny—and now I have two dimes!" Deena said. "I'm going to buy a present for Mom's birthday."

Dad reached into his pocket. "Here's a nickel to go with your two dimes. How much money do you have now?"

"20 cents plus 5 cents equals 25 cents," said Deena. "That's the same as a quarter!"

"Would you like to trade your two dimes and one nickel for this quarter?" asked Dad.

"Yes! Thanks, Dad!" said Deena.

10¢ + 10¢ + 5¢ = 25¢

Deena could hardly wait to show her quarter to Grandma and Grandpa. They were coming for supper.

Deena set the table.

She stacked her books.

She changed her clothes.

Finally, she heard the doorbell.

"Grandma! Grandpa!" Deena said. "I found a lucky penny—and now I have a quarter!"

"Wow!" said Grandpa. "How did that happen?"

"Like this," Deena said. "I found a lucky penny. Mrs. Green turned it into a nickel. Sam turned it into a dime. Amy turned it into two dimes. And Dad turned them into a quarter!"

"What are you going to do with your quarter?" asked Grandpa.

"I'm saving it to buy a present for Mom's birthday," answered Deena.

"Then you may need more than twenty-five cents," said Grandpa. "Why don't I give you another quarter?"

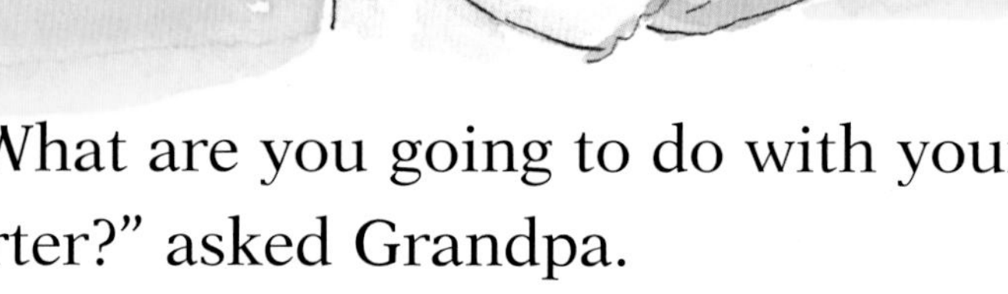

"Thanks, Grandpa!" Deena said. "25 cents plus 25 cents equals 50 cents! That's half of a dollar!"

25¢ + 25¢ = 50¢

"Deena," Grandma said, "will you let me try a magic trick with your two quarters?"

A magic trick? With her two quarters? Deena wasn't sure. But then she saw the twinkle in Grandma's eyes.

"Okay, Grandma," said Deena. "But please don't lose my fifty cents!"

Grandma took the two quarters. She dropped them down into her big purse.

"Abracadabra!" said Grandma. She waved her hand over the purse.

Then Grandma reached down deep inside her purse. Slowly, she pulled out her hand.

"Four quarters!" Deena cried.

First, Grandma put three quarters in Deena's hand.

"Now let's see how much money you have," Grandma said.

"25 cents plus 25 cents plus 25 cents equals 75 cents," said Deena.

25¢ + 25¢ + 25¢ = 75¢

Then Grandma put the last quarter in Deena's hand.

"75 cents plus 25 cents equals 100 cents," said Deena. "And 100 cents equals ONE DOLLAR!"

She gave her grandma a big hug.

"Would you like to trade your four quarters for a dollar bill?" asked Grandma.

"Yes, please!" said Deena. "Now do I have enough money to buy Mom a present?"

"Yes, you do," said Grandma. "Tomorrow I'll take you to the Dollar Store. They have lots of things for a dollar."

25¢ + 25¢ + 25¢ + 25¢ = $1.00

By now dinner was ready. Dad peeked around the kitchen door. "I think I hear Mom coming," he said.

Sure enough, Mom walked in.

"Mom! Guess what?" Deena said. "I found lucky penny today!"

"Lucky you!" said Mom. "What are you oing to do with it?"

Deena couldn't help smiling. "It's a secret," ie said.

That night Deena thought about her lucky penny and how it grew from a penny to a dollar...from one cent to one hundred cents.

It was just like Mrs. Green's rhyme.

Find a penny.
Pick it up.
All the day you'll have good luck.

Today had been a *very* lucky day. And tomorrow would be even better. Tomorrow she would buy her mom a birthday present!

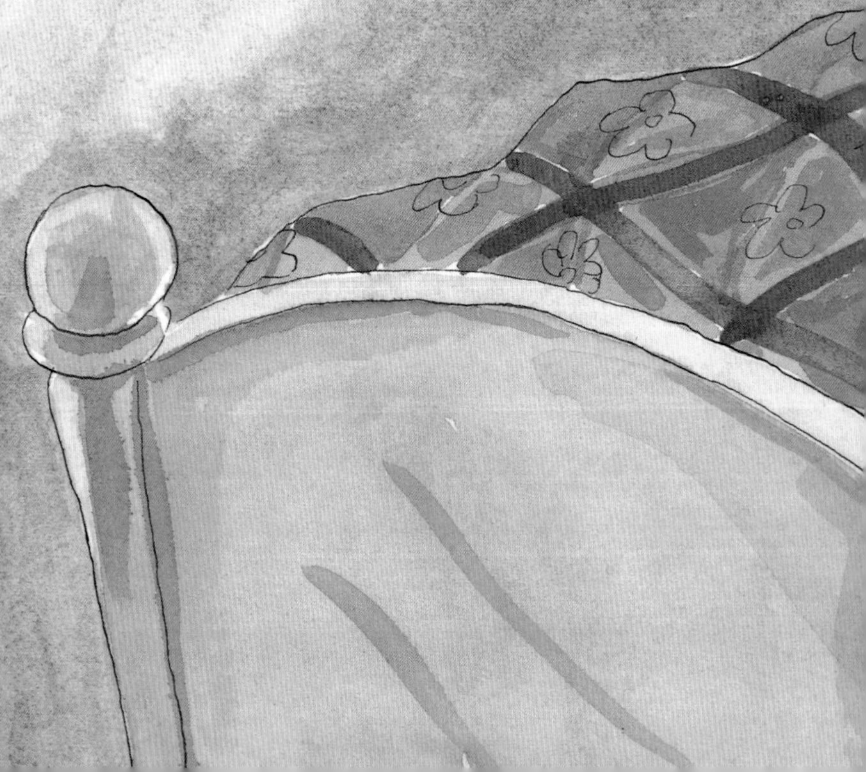

DOLLAR $1 STORE
Pet
Treat

Money Chart

				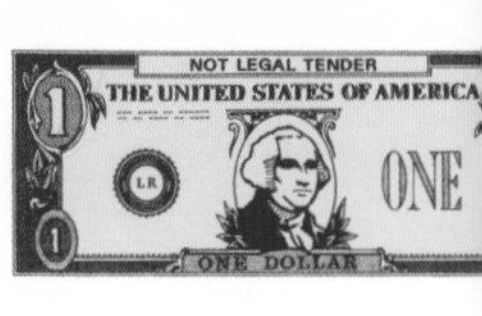
penny 1 cent 1¢	nickel 5 cents 5¢	dime 10 cents 10¢	quarter 25 cents 25¢	dollar 100 cents 100¢ or $1.00

Here are two ways to make each amount.
Can you think of other ways?

5¢	5 cents	1 nickel	5 pennies
10¢	 10 cents	2 nickels	1 nickel, 5 pennie
20¢	20 cents	2 dimes	1 dime, 2 nickels
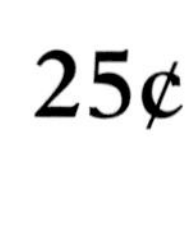 **25¢**	 25 cents	2 dimes, 1 nickel	5 nickels
 **50¢**	 50 cents	2 quarters	5 dimes
 **100¢**	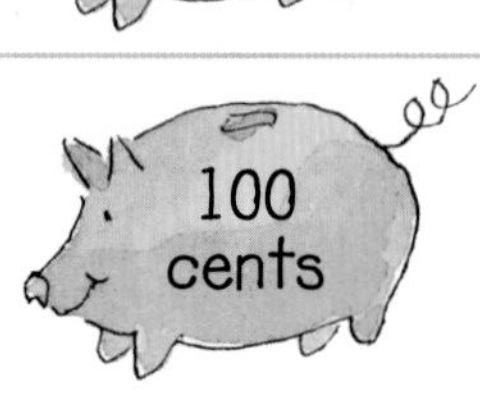 100 cents	4 quarters	8 dimes, 4 nickel